TROLL STINKS

JEANNE WILLIS

TONY ROSS

ANDERSEN PRESS

There was a little billy goat
who found a mobile phone
just like the one the farmer lost
and kept it for his own.

ne'

FOR
FRANCISCO
JAVIER ORTIZ
J.W.

He hid it from his
mum and dad.
He knew that they
would say,

"You're not old enough for that!"
and take the phone away.

Off he trotted down
the lane to show his
best friend, Cyril.
They played a funny
game and took a photo
of a squirrel.

They found a tatty scarecrow and
they wore his coat and scarf.
Then Cyril took a selfie and
that made the two goats laugh.

They listened to some music and then filmed a crazy cow. "Hilarious!" said Cyril. "Billy, what shall we do now?"

Little Billy thought and said,
"Let's make a funny call!"
He scrolled through Farmer's contacts
while they hid behind a wall.

Billy called his brother
and he burped a little tune.
Then Cyril rang his sister,
whooping like a big baboon.

They scrolled through all the names
then Billy's eyes lit up with glee.
"I've got Troll's number here!" he said. "Oh, what a laugh, yippee!"

"Grandpa Gruff says trolls are bad.
If one should ever meet us
when we cross the old stone bridge,
he told me it would eat us!"
"Let's send a message," Billy said.
"We'll sort out Troll from here
for thinking that it owns that bridge
and filling goats with fear."

"What shall we say?" asked Cyril.
Little Bill began to text:

GET OFF THE BRIDGE!
YOU STINK!

he typed. "Cyril,
your turn next."

Cyril took the mobile
and he texted:

TROLL IS DUMB!

YOUR DAD HAS GOT
A WARTY NOSE.

A MOOSE LOOKS
LIKE YOUR MUM.

The goats grew even bolder
as Bill said with a laugh,
"I bet Troll's got an ugly mug –
let's take its photograph!"

They trotted past the meadow
and across the spooky wood,
and found the reeking riverbank
where the stone bridge stood.

"I've set the phone to camera,"
said Billy with a grin.
"When Troll pokes out its
ugly head, we'll both burst in.
Then you can take its picture
(you must do it in a flash)."
"And then?" gasped Cyril.
Billy giggled, "Off we dash!"

They waited for the moment,
then they entered, bold and brave.
But to their horror, a big bad troll...

... was **NOT** inside the cave.
Just a tiny, frightened troll
who looked as sweet as pie,
with tears rolling down her face.
What had made her cry?

"Someone sent me horrid texts!"
she wept upon her bed.
"What wicked monsters would do that?"
"Um... us?" the bad goats said.

"Why do you hate me so?" she sobbed.
"I've never once hurt you.
Not every troll eats goats, you know.
We trolls have feelings too!"

"I'm truly sorry," Cyril said.
Then Bill said, "So am I."

"We're really silly billy goats, forgive us. Please don't cry." The goat kids hung their heads in shame. They put the phone away...

... and played a game called Making Friends,
which everyone should play!